Miko's
Muzzy Mess

Books by Robert Elmer

www.elmerbooks.org

ASTROKIDS

PROMISE OF ZION

ADVENTURES DOWN UNDER

THE YOUNG UNDERGROUND

ROBERT ELMER

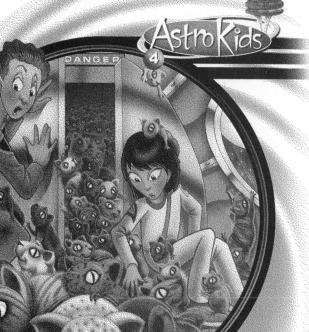

AstroKids

DANGER

Miko's Muzzy Mess

BETHANY BACKYARD®

www.bethanyhouse.com

Miko's Muzzy Mess
Copyright © 2001
Robert Elmer

Cover and text illustrations by Paul Turnbaugh
Cover design by Lookout Design Group, Inc.

Unless otherwise identified, Scripture quotations are from the *International Children's Bible, New Century Version,* copyright © 1986, 1988 by Word Publishing, Dallas, Texas 75039. Used by permission.

Published by Bethany House Publishers
11400 Hampshire Avenue South
Bloomington, Minnesota 55438
www.bethanyhouse.com

Bethany House Publishers is a Division of
Baker Book House Company, Grand Rapids, Michigan.

Printed in the United States of America

Library of Congress Cataloging-in-Publication Data

Elmer, Robert.
   Miko's muzzy mess / by Robert Elmer.
      p. cm. — (AstroKids ; 4)
Summary: Things quickly get out of hand on *CLEO-7* after Miko feeds chocolate to a pair of hybrid critters called "muzzies."
   ISBN 0-7642-2359-3 (pbk.)
   [1. Space stations—Fiction. 2. Christian life—Fiction. 3. Science fiction.] I. Title.
   PZ7.E4794 Mi 2001
   [Fic]—dc21

                                     2001001322

To all the Y.W.I. kids—

you know who you are!

THIS STORY WAS ENGINEERED AND WRITTEN BY...

Robert

Freckles

ROBERT ELMER is an Earth-based author who writes for life-forms all over the solar system. He was born the year after the first *Sputnik* satellite was launched, and grew up while Russia and the United States were racing to put a man on the moon. Today, Robert and his family live in a muzzy-free zone about ninety-three million miles from the sun, with their dog, Freckles (who would be scared to death of a muzzy if he ever saw one).

Contents

✳ ✳ ✳

MEET THE
AstroKids

Lamar "Buzz" Bright

Show the way, Buzz! The leader of the AstroKids always has a great plan. He also loves Jupiter ice cream.

Daphne "DeeBee" Ortiz

DeeBee's the brains of the bunch—she can build or fix almost anything. But, suffering satellites, don't tell her she's a "GEEN-ius"!

Theodore "Tag" Ortiz

Yeah, DeeBee's little brother, Tag, always tags along. Count on him to say something silly at just the wrong time. He's in orbit.

Kumiko "Miko" Sato

Everybody likes Miko the stowaway. They just don't know how she got to be a karate master, or how she knows so much about space shuttles.

Vladimir "Mir" Chekhov

So his dad's the station commander and Mir usually gets his way? Give him a break! He's trying. And whatever he did, it was probably just a joke.

Invasion of the
1 Plasma Blobs

✳ ✳ ✳

"They're coming through the ceiling!" screamed the first officer of the *Pluto Explorer*. A green blob of plasma dropped onto his arm and sizzled.

Tzzssss.

"Aii-EEE!"

It was too late for the crew of the star cruiser. They should have known something like this would happen. They were on a five-year mission to explore new worlds, after all. To boldly go where no one had gone before.

So much for space exploring. The horrible green plasma blob from Planet X-20 had eaten through the outside skin of the ship. No one could stop it.

"This is the end, Captain Quirk!" someone gasped.

"That would be highly illogical," said another officer.

"What does 'illogical' mean?" Tag asked. He was not traveling through space on the *Pluto Explorer*. He was just watching the ship and its crew on a holo-vid.

"Shh!" answered DeeBee. She tapped her little brother on the shoulder. "*You're* illogical."

"Oh? Well, that green stuff reminds me of when someone sneezes," whispered Tag.

The other boys watching the 3-D holo-vid laughed.

Boys? I mean Buzz, the leader of the AstroKids, and Mir. He's the space-station commander's son.

"Grow up, Tag." It was DeeBee's job to keep her brother in line. "Miko and I are trying to watch."

Miko. That would be me.

"Saw-ree," Tag giggled. "It's just too funny."

"*Star Wreck* isn't supposed to be funny."

"It's snot?" Tag hooted at his rude joke while the plasma globs dropped all around us. That is how holo-vids are—the picture and sound are all around you, just like you are really there.

Tzzzsss. A blob branded Captain Quirk on the hand.

Double ouch.

Not even Tag giggled at that. I could see him pull his own hand back in the green light.

Now, please don't ask me how Tag went from nose-blowing jokes to shaking in his chair. But his teeth began to chatter as if he had just stuck his finger in one of *CLEO-7*'s power generators.

Tzzzsss. Another plasma blob connected. I covered my eyes. You might have done the same thing, if you had been there.

I'm very sorry, but by that time, my stomach was not feeling too well.

"Go to warp drive, Snotty!" cried Captain Quirk. "Get us out of here."

"Ach, I'm sorry, Captain," a Scottish voice answered. "But we've a wee problem in the engine room. The blobs are oozin' through the ceiling, they are."

Tzzzsss.

I got up and slipped out the door.

"Snotty? Snotty?" the captain called with his last breath.

"Miko? Miko?" DeeBee followed me out into the hallway. "Are you okay?"

I should tell you the truth: I was not okay. My stomach felt upside-down, inside out. And my dinner was ready to . . . But no, I don't want to be rude; I will spare you the details. All I could think of were the blobs coming through the walls.

"They're not going to get me," I whispered.

"Miko?" DeeBee caught up to me. "It wasn't that scary, was it? It was just a holo-vid."

I shook my head. DeeBee was the nicest person I knew. But she did not understand.

"I'm sorry," I told her. "I . . . uh—"

"Don't apologize." DeeBee patted me on the shoulder. "Besides, nobody's going to get you. Buzz and I, we'll make sure of it!"

She put up her fists and showed me her muscles, like a champion arm wrestler.

I tried to smile and not look so worried. (Not always so easy for me!)

"Maybe I just needed some fresh air," I told her.

About a minute later, so did Tag. Zero-G, the dog, hurried out next, his tail tucked between his legs. Even Buzz joined us.

"Hmm." DeeBee smiled.

Tag held his face in his hands, and Buzz's eyes were twice their normal size. Both boys looked pale.

"Whoaa," groaned Tag. "That was gross."

"Mercy." Buzz leaned against the wall.

So. I was not the only one who had to leave. They couldn't say it was because I was a girl. That made me feel a little better.

But not much.

"You left Mir in there?" DeeBee asked the boys.

"Hey, guys?" The door to the holo-room swooshed open and Mir Chekhov peeked out. His wavy blond hair stood up straight, and he was breathing hard. "Buzz? Where did you go, buddy?"

"Over here." Buzz waved his hand.

Mir slicked down his hair—you know, as if

nothing were wrong. But I saw his wide-eyed look.

"So, how'd you like the holo-vid?" Mir shuffled up to join us. "Pretty tame, huh? Just a few gross parts."

A few bad parts were enough to ruin the whole thing, I thought. Just like a few little meteors could put a hole in a space shuttle.

Mir went on. "I'd love to stay for the rest of it, of course, but I have—"

"Mir—" began DeeBee.

"No, hey, it's all right." Buzz put up his hand. "I understand if you can't stay for the ending. I've got some stuff I need to do for my dad. Gotta go."

Ah, Buzz, the Master of AstroCool. I smiled— until something brushed up against the back of my neck.

A plasma blob?

"AHHHHHH!"

I screamed.

Mir screamed.

We all screamed.

They Came From the Ceiling

2

* * *

Everyone screamed when the blob attacked me.

"Hi-YAH!" I grunted and spun around. But the blob had disappeared.

QUESTION 01:

"Hi-yah"? What language is that?

ANSWER 01:

Think of when someone shines a bright light in your face. You blink. You can't help it. It's the same when someone scares me: I bend my knees and put up my hands, karate-style. *Hi-yah!* To me, karate is like blinking. I'm always practicing . . . it comes in handy when you are being chased.

QUESTION 02:

You've been chased? Why would anybody chase you?

ANSWER 02:

I was afraid you would ask. (Heavy sigh.) You know I'm from Moon Colony 2, right? I suppose you also know I had to hide in a shuttle to get to *CLEO-7*. Sorry, but that's all I can tell you . . . for now.

"Miko?" Buzz asked. "What's wrong?"

Something moved above our heads. It was bright green and coming out of the ceiling. I started to worry about my life. (DeeBee tells me I worry about my life too much. She says the Bible says not to worry.)

"Watch out!" yelled Tag. He grabbed me. DeeBee ducked, her hands over her head. Buzz dived for cover. Mir tried running, but slipped and fell.

"Everybody stay calm!" ordered Buzz.

That was easy for him to say. He was not

standing right under the blob. Right *smack* under-
neath, DeeBee would say.

As for me, I knew my bare hands would not
work against a blob. They had not worked for Captain Quirk. I opened my eyes bravely to face the
end.

I expected . . . an evil hiss. The end.

I heard . . . a sweet gurgling sound. If you have
ever heard a pigeon, you know what I'm talking
about. It sounded sort of like . . .

"Rrrroooo?"

Want to hear it again?

"Rrrroooo?"

I put down my hands and began to breathe
again. (Sound effect: loud sigh of relief.) You will
be glad to know this blob did not look like the blob
from *Star Wreck*'s "Invasion of the Blob." Not at
all.

It was green, to be sure, but it was no blob.

Picture a furry green hamster. (You know, with
cute little black eyes and tiny ears you can almost
see through.)

Then picture a nice, fuzzy caterpillar. (I'm

talking about the kind you let crawl on your hand because it tickles.)

This animal was something in-between: part cute hamster, part fuzzy caterpillar.

But there was more than one creature. The other one had brushed the back of my neck when it fell to the floor. We didn't see that one, at first, as we watched its friend doing chin-ups on a ceiling air vent. He was barely hanging on with his tiny pink paws.

And then *plop*. He landed on the floor next to his friend.

"Is anybody going to pick them up?" DeeBee asked. She was never afraid of anything. Not like me.

Afraid or not, I got down on my knees. Because when animals need help, it is no good to be afraid. Besides, they looked cute.

"Come here, little friends," I whispered.

They could crawl quite fast. "Rrrrooo?" They sounded like cats purring as I scratched their little backs. If you have ever heard a cat purring, you

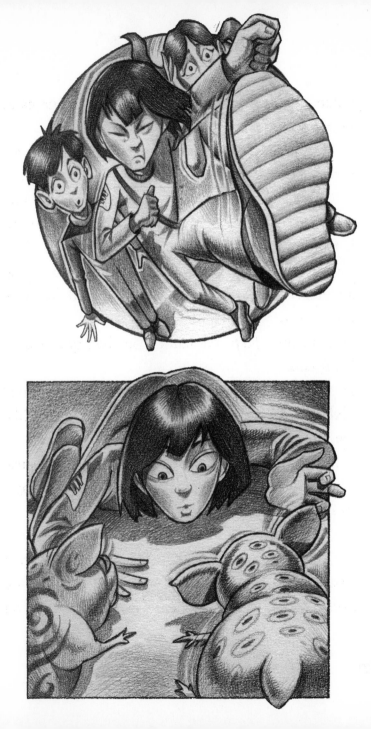

know what that does to people: They always smile. This I guarantee.

"Aww, he's cute." DeeBee bent down and started to stroke the creature's extra-fuzzy fur, too. Pretty soon, everyone was petting them.

"I think they're stowaways," said Mir.

Stowaways. Just like me.

We had a pretty good idea where they had come from: a Galaxian Trader's ship that had visited *CLEO-7* a few weeks before. (But that's another story!)

"Please don't squish them," I said. But I need not have worried. Because the more everyone stroked these two creatures, the more the animals purred.

I decided then that I liked them. When I held one in my hand, the other hopped up, too.

"I'll bet they're hungry," said Mir. Leave it to Mir to think about food. Mir is always eating and never gets fat. But perhaps he was right this time. So we all checked our pockets for something to feed them.

"What about this?" asked Tag. He held out a

disgusting, half-chewed piece of pale purple Super Galaxy Gum.

"No, Tag." DeeBee shook her head.

But she was too late. One of the little animals snapped the gum out of Tag's fingers.

If you didn't scream at this point, you don't know about Super Galaxy Gum. It lets you blow a bubble a meter wide. That is one big bubble.

"Get it out of his mouth!" yelled Buzz.

"It's going to choke him!" Mir hollered. And he was right.

This was not funny!

Chocolate Boo-Boo

It took a lot of yelling and screaming to get the gum out of the little animal's mouth. Actually, it dropped out after I held him upside down and shook him a little.

I tried to be gentle, and I felt bad about scaring him. After that, I held the little creature still for a while. I stroked his soft green fur until he purred again.

And then I remembered the Blast-Off Chocolate Bar in my pocket.

QUESTION 03:

Blast-Off Chocolate?

ANSWER 03:

Blast-Off Chocolate Bars start out as small as your little finger, but get bigger and bigger in your mouth. I have learned to nibble my Blast-Off bars with care. Only once did I put the whole thing in my mouth, and I was sorry for that.

Anyway, I had saved this Blast-Off bar to eat on the trip from the moon to the space station. Then I forgot about it. Now, as soon as I unwrapped it with my teeth, the creatures sat right up and opened their tiny mouths.

They were hungry!

"I think they like chocolate." I held up the candy.

"Uh, Miko." Buzz held up his finger. "I don't know if that's such a good idea."

"Why not?" I could not see any problem. "They look hungry."

"Yeah, but chocolate? Everyone knows chocolate isn't good for animals. Especially not Blast-Off bars. I wouldn't, if I were you."

I confess I was not listening to Buzz. I was watching the animals instead. They looked at me with their cute black eyes, begging for a bite. Who could say no? Not I. I broke the bar in two and held it out to them.

"Here you go, friends. Just one nibble. There. I'm sure it will not hurt anything."

A little closer, and . . .

The Blast-Off bars disappeared. Even worse, my fingers disappeared, too!

Both gone!

"Oh dear!" I cried.

"Whoa!" Tag leaned in to see. "Did they want your hands, too?"

I pulled my fingers back from the hungry animals' rough little mouths and counted.

"Eight, nine, ten . . ." (Sound effect: a loud sigh of relief!)

"You do not have to worry about fingers." DeeBee's homemade watermelon-sized silver drone, MAC, swooped through a door and hovered into the room. He must have finished recharging his power cells. "A muzzo-lumpiriri has teeth, but they do not eat meat. Especially not human fingers."

"Good thing." Tag counted his fingers, too.

Probably just to make sure.

"What did you say?" I asked. "A muzzy-what?" (Do not worry about saying that word yourself at home. I couldn't, either.)

"These are two muzzo-lumpiriri, named for the scientist who first raised them in his lab at Moon Colony 3, Dr. Muzzolump. He was the first to cross a hamster and a caterpillar. He had some problems, though."

"Wow." Tag whistled. "Wonder if they had a lot of chocolate to feed 'em. Looks as if they like that."

"Chocolate?" A couple of MAC's red warning lights blinked on. "Explain, please."

"Oh, they looked hungry, so Miko fed them a little—"

"Please do not tell me you fed these animals chocolate." More red lights. He must not have seen what I had done. To tell the truth, I don't think I would have told him.

"It was just going to be one little nibble," I whispered.

"Warning, warning." MAC began to spin. He

was going to pop a fuse, I was sure of it. "My sensors tell me the muzzo-lumpiriri cannot eat chocolate without . . ."

"Without what?" Now I had to know.

"Without . . ." A puff of smoke escaped from under a patch on MAC's side.

Please, not again! We had seen this kind of thing before. The drone would get excited about something—a spaceball game score, or news about an incoming shuttle, whatever. No matter how hard he spun or how much his lights blinked, he simply could not say what he wanted to say. You must realize how sorry I felt for the poor machine.

Phooot!

"Oh man," DeeBee groaned when her drone went dark and stopped spinning. "Another fuse to fix. That's the third time in three days."

It was nothing serious, but I still wanted to know what MAC was talking about. Now that would have to wait. I held the two "muzzies" in my hand. They looked very happy and not at all hungry.

I looked at DeeBee. "Do you think your father—"

"Sure, he will, IMHO." She meant "In My Humble Opinion." DeeBee talks that way sometimes. "He let us keep a kitten once, when we were little. These will be a lot less trouble."

I dearly hoped so. But I was not so sure.

Two, Four, Six, 4 Eight . . .

* * *

QUESTION 04:

Wait a minute. Before we start a new chapter, you have to explain something. You said you're from Moon Colony 2 and you hid in a shuttle to get to *CLEO*-7. Where do you stay now?

ANSWER 04:

Well . . . DeeBee's family has let me stay with them—at least until they can figure out where I belong. I share a room with DeeBee. I am a stowaway, remember? Please don't ask about that sort of thing again.

QUESTION 05:

Why not?

ANSWER 05:

Could we change the subject . . . please?

Thanks! New subject: When I woke up the next morning, what was the first thing I had to check? The muzzies!

I had put them to bed the night before inside a cozy box in the corner of the bedroom, with a bowl of water and an old sock of Tag's for comfort. (A clean one, of course—Tag's feet get pretty stinky.)

Now, everyone else in the Ortiz living compartment was still sleeping, but I rolled up my anti-grav mat and tiptoed to see the muzzies.

QUESTION 06:

Not so fast. I've never heard of an anti-grav mat.

ANSWER 06:

Oh dear. An "antigravity" mat is a sleeping mat that floats about a meter off the ground. They are quite comfy and much better than sleeping on the floor.

Anyway, my two muzzy pets were already chirping in their cute muzzy voices. You should have heard them.

"Rrrrooo? Rrrrooo? Rrrrooo!"

You can probably imagine the sound by this time. But they were a little noisier than the day before.

"RRRROOOOO!"

I'm sorry; what I said is not quite true. They were not a little noisier than the night before.

They were a *lot* noisier.

"Hey, little friends," I whispered. I peeked over the edge and started to reach down to pet them. But I had to stop.

I gasped.

Oh dear.

Oh my.

Oh muzzy!

"Rrrrooo? Rrrrooo?"

I looked around to make sure DeeBee had not heard, then took another peek. I am afraid we were not talking about just two muzzies anymore.

I counted again to make sure. I would not want

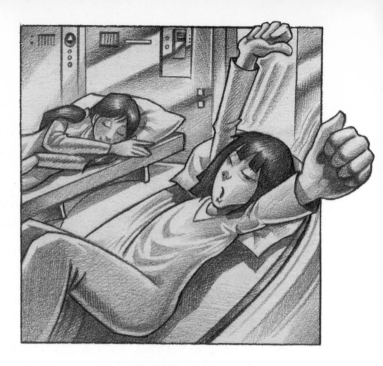

to mislead anyone. Eight, nine, ten . . .

Fifteen of them. No, make that twenty! Have you ever tried to count that many muzzies? It is fair to say they knew how to wriggle.

The strange thing was, none of them looked like babies. They were all nearly as big as the first two muzzies! Do not ask me how, but they must have grown very quickly.

They were crawling up the sides of the box, climbing all over one another. That made counting even tougher. But worse than that, one of them had already chewed a hole in the side of the box.

"How are your muzzy things doing?" DeeBee wiped the sleep from her eyes and rolled over on her bunk. She waved her hand in the direction of the wall, and it started to glow. (That was not magic. That was how the light panels in DeeBee's room worked.)

How were my muzzy things doing? What could I tell her?

"They are doing great. Really great."

Better than great, I thought as I plugged up the hole in the side with Tag's sock and put a lid on the box. No telling how many had crawled through the hole. I was afraid by that time that a herd of young muzzies was loose in the station.

Who knew how many? Maybe a few, maybe dozens? And if they had chewed through the side of the box, who knew what else they could chew?

I worried. (You already know I am good at that.)

This was turning into a disaster.

A Muzzy Mess!

Nightmare, Part One

A few days later, DeeBee and I still had not found any of the missing muzzies. I had to tell her about them, you see. We now had about two hundred in a big box in our workshop. (I am sorry I cannot tell you exactly how many there were. Each time we tried to add them up, we counted more!)

I hoped that maybe no muzzies had escaped from my box, after all. It was a nice thought for me to think. Only trouble was, it wasn't true. I found out on Day 05 of the Muzzy Mess, at 0700—that's short for seven o'clock in the morning.

"Hey, look what I found under my bed!" Tag came tumbling into DeeBee's and my room without knocking. Most times, that would get him a pillow in the face from DeeBee. But this time was different. He held up double handfuls of fuzzy blue and yellow muzzies.

"Under your bed?" DeeBee and I asked at the same time. We knew what Tag kept under there. Not just disgusting old gum, but grimy Space Pops, half-nibbled Tart-ee Stars, and stale Choco-Planets. Which reminded me of . . .

The Wise Space Sayings of Miko Sato, Number 01

"Cleanliness is next to . . .
 . . .chocolate (in the dictionary)."

"Yeah," said Tag. "They ate up all my candy stash. Wrappers and everything!"

"Serves you right for keeping all that junky candy under your bed," said DeeBee. "Is that all of them?" She meant muzzies.

Tag shrugged.

"I'll get another box," I told them as I went for the door.

Whoops! I almost bowled into MAC as he whooshed in. Buzz and Mir were right behind him. They must have found out about Tag's muzzies, too.

"I was afraid something bad would happen," fumed MAC. His red warning lights were blinking again.

"What do you mean?" Tag asked.

"I mean, we have a big problem," answered MAC. "And Miko's chocolate was the catalyst."

"What kind of list?" Tag didn't get it. "A cat list?"

"No, a catalyst is a *starter.*"

Mir scratched his head. "So you think Miko's chocolate made them start . . . ah, making more muzzies?"

"It wasn't supposed to. Chocolate usually makes animals very sick. But this chocolate made them multiply."

Multiply? That sounds hard. But you can do the arithmetic. MAC told us to double the number two. Make it twice as big. Then do it again. So two muzzies become four. Four become eight, then sixteen. That's *multiplying.* And take my word for it. It adds up really quickly.

As Tag would say, *huge-mongous.*

"Hey." Tag finally got the math lesson. "This is going to be fun."

"Not when you reach 532 billion hungry creatures," said MAC. "I believe that's enough to fill at least three space stations the size of *CLEO-7*."

"How soon will that be?" I checked the box. It had not taken long for us to go from two to two hundred.

"At this rate. . . ." A couple of MAC's lights blinked. "Forty-seven days, fourteen hours . . ."

He started spinning. Another red light came on.

"No, perhaps forty-*eight* days, twelve hours, or . . ."

"It's okay, MAC!" DeeBee tapped a button on the side of her drone. "Don't sweat it. We just have to get rid of all the chocolate, all over the station. Just in case more muzzies are loose."

"No more *chocolate*?" wailed Tag.

Oh dear. Poor Tag. But DeeBee was right. We could not have Tag leaving any more leftovers under his bed.

"One-teen minutes and . . . twenty-ten seconds," MAC went on.

"Will they ever stop making more muzzies?" DeeBee asked.

"I don't know." MAC finally settled down. "But I will find out."

I closed my eyes. I had meant to give them only a little bite of chocolate. I should have listened to Buzz when he told me not to. Never mind the muzzies getting out and eating Tag's candy. This mess started with me. None of it would have happened if I had not fed them chocolate. It was really all my fault.

As Mir would say, things were getting worser and worser.

"No one is going to send me back," I turned away and whispered to myself. And I tried my best not to cry. "No one."

DeeBee must have heard me. "What are you talking about?"

I hated to cry in front of people. But when the tears launched, I could not stop them.

"I'm sorry," I told the rest of the AstroKids. "Really I am. I should have listened to Buzz."

"Nobody's blaming you, Miko. It's not a big

deal." Buzz tried to make me feel better.

I liked that. But I knew better. "Your *parents* will all blame me, though," I told them. "And then—"

Whoops. I had almost let slip my secret.

"And then what?" asked Tag.

I buttoned my lip.

"Tell us, Miko." DeeBee again. "We're all AstroKids, remember?"

She was right. Who else could I tell, if not my friends?

I took a deep breath. "When they find out what I did," I wiped my eyes, "they'll send me back to Moon Colony 2."

"I thought you didn't have any family there," said Mir.

I nodded. "My father has been on a deep-space mission since I was a baby. I haven't heard from him for a long time. After my mother . . . died, I was put in the Apollo Children's Home."

It felt better to finally tell someone about that place. I could not keep it a secret forever.

"Was it that bad?" DeeBee put her hand on my shoulder.

"Worse. I just had to get away. And now, if . . ."

I did not want to start crying again. DeeBee would call it *blubbering*.

"We all want you here, Miko," Buzz spoke up. "We're not going to let anyone send you back."

That sounded good.

"All we have to do is find a good home for the muzzies!" Tag made it sound like a game. "Then nobody will be mad at you—or us."

Well, I was glad *he* thought it would be so simple. But how many muzzies were we talking about?

Two hundred?

Two thousand?

More?

"And *you*, Miko." DeeBee held me by the shoulders. "You just stop worrying so much, okay? You won't live longer by worrying about it."

I thought I had heard DeeBee say that before. Then I remembered. "Jesus said that, right?"

"Yeah." She nodded. "It's in my Bible. I guess the basic idea is . . . God's got it under control."

I hoped He did. Because I knew one thing:

I sure did not.

The Invasion
6 Begins

* * *

Day 06 of the Muzzy Mess looked pretty good. We had found fifty more muzzies in Tag's closet. No more. Still, we had to keep looking, just to make sure. Because . . .

The Wise Space Sayings of Miko Sato, Number 02

"The early bird . . .
. . . catches the muzzy."

In the meantime, we had to do something about the thousands of muzzies in our shop.

"I must tell you that I do not enjoy this one bit!" Zero-G sniffed the corner, then turned away and sneezed. "Just because I'm a dog, doesn't mean I'm a bloodhound. I don't know why you can't use an e-sniffer."

Remember that Zero-G talks. Well, not like you and I talk. He thinks doggie thoughts, and the mind-to-voice box on his collar picks up those thoughts and chooses words to match. Understand?

"I'm sorry about all the sniffing, Zero-G," I told him as I followed along behind. "But this is the last place we have to search. And no one else has your nose."

"A good thing. I wouldn't want to share it with anyone else."

"Oh, I mean . . . no one else smells as good as you do."

"Thank you so much! Perhaps it was what I rolled in yesterday. And I *never* take those horrid sonic showers, you know."

QUESTION 07:
   Wait! A dog that takes *showers*?
ANSWER 07:
   Not exactly. A sonic shower "showers" you with sound (that's the "sonic" part). No

water. The sound waves are hyper-transformed, so you don't hear them, but you feel them. The shower gently cleans you with sound waves. Ahhh . . .

"I know dogs don't take showers, Zero-G. That is not what I meant. I meant no one else can smell—with their nose—as well as you can."

"Ah, you meant *well*, I see. Why didn't you say so?" The little dog sniffed in a corner.

"Sure, I meant *well*." Professor Zero-G had me up a grammar tree. Zero-G didn't smell *good*, but he smelled *well*.

"But Mistress Miko, you can *hear* the little creatures almost as well as I can."

He had a point. I petted the muzzy on my shoulder to make him purr. Maybe that is why we kids all liked them so much—all the purring.

"It's okay, Wuzzy." That's what I called mine. Wuzzy Muzzy. He had one droopy ear, which is how I could tell him apart from all the others. His fur was a very pretty shade of green, and he had the cutest black eyes you've ever seen. "No one is going to hurt you. We'll find your friends."

But we had to find every last one of them, wherever they were hiding. Before they turned into a million-zillion muzzies.

Before something terrible happened.

Worry, worry, worry!

But this time, I *really* had something to worry about. Especially since Mir had told us his father was getting tired of all the muzzy trouble. He was talking about getting rid of them.

Hint: He was not talking about finding them happy families and new homes!

"Here, muzzy, muzzy!" I called.

"Game's over, muzzies!" yelled Tag. "Come out, come out wherever you are!"

"Ah-eeee!" someone screamed in the dining hall. We heard it as if the person screaming were standing next to us, even though we were out in the hallway and the door was closed.

"What was that?" Tag asked.

We ran to find out.

Swoo— The dining-room door opened halfway.

We hurried over to where the screaming person had dropped her meal.

"It's okay," I told her. "Just a muzzy. He won't hurt you."

I picked the poor creature up off the floor before someone stepped on him. He was blue, too, just like the screaming tekky's coveralls.

"But h-he came out of the digital food copier!" huffed the woman. "He just dropped onto my plate."

"It's today's blue-plate special." I held up the little fellow and tried to smile. He looked okay.

"This is strange." DeeBee stared into the opening in the wall where the food comes out. She knew the DFC copied only food, like tacos and milkshakes. Not living animals, like muzzies.

Then I had an idea.

"Did you order chocolate?" I asked the tech.

"Well . . ." The tech looked a little guilty, I thought. "Just a bite."

"M-hmm." I nodded and pushed the Repeat button on the wall above the food copier. That would give me the same thing the woman had ordered.

But instead of a dark chocolate bar, out popped an orange muzzy. And instead of chocolate-covered raisins . . .

Plop! Plop!

Muzzies number three and four! A pair of yellow muzzies. They were purring, saying something to each other, I guessed.

"What are they doing inside the DFC?" Tag wondered aloud.

"Looking for more chocolate." If this was a puzzle, I had almost figured it out. I started to loosen the wall panel to check inside the copier. "They must have good noses, like Zero-G. Maybe they can smell chocolate."

Yikes! I should have known better. Because when I pulled off the cover just a little—

"Ah-eeeeee!" The tech let loose another scream—even louder than the one before. "It's an *invasion!*"

7 Piled to the Sky ✳ ✳ ✳

Now, as you know, adults get excited easily—sometimes for the silliest things. But this was different. None of us had ever been ankle-deep in wiggling, purring muzzies before. They just kept pouring out from the DFC.

"Do you still want me to keep sniffing for those little creatures, Mistress Miko?" Zero-G was almost buried under a pile of fuzzy blue, yellow, orange, green, and red muzzies.

"Not right now, Zero-G. I think we found them."

Or they found us. We counted at least . . .

"Five thousand, two hundred and three." Mir dropped another one into our collecting box an hour later. We had stacked boxes to the ceiling of our shop. "Five thousand, two hundred and four. Five thousand, two hundred and—"

And that was just the start.

Dee-DOOP! Mir's wrist interface *dee-dooped*.

"Okay, sure," Mir told the man that had popped up to talk to him. "Lab 03? We'll be right there."

This was getting serious. Mir's dad had ordered all chocolate be locked up. And we AstroKids were working extra hard to collect the muzzy "invaders" all over the station, before all the adults went crazy.

Why us? I had already explained that to the rest of the AstroKids.

"This is *my* hunt," I had told them. "I'm going to find these muzzies, if it's the last thing I do. *Before* they get hurt."

"What do you mean, hurt?" Mir asked.

"Didn't some of the tekkies say they were going to open a shuttle hangar and shoo them out?" answered Buzz.

I put up my hands. "That's just what I mean! We really have to find them, now more than ever!"

"Yeah, but all of them?" Tag asked. "There's a million-gabillion of them."

I nodded. It might sound silly, but I really felt

for these little animals. After all, they were stow-aways.

"Here's another load for you." A tech came in with another bagful and poured them on the floor. "But I still think we should dump 'em—"

He must have seen me scowl. He shrugged his shoulders.

"Whatever. Just keep 'em out of my lab from now on."

We hurried down the hallway to lab 03 a few minutes later. DeeBee and Buzz were off in another part of the station, collecting still more muzzies.

"Muzzies in the hallways," I muttered. "Muzzies in the shops."

"Muzzies in the gardens," added Mir. "Muzzies in the walls." He started snapping his fingers in time to a tune he had just made up. "Muzzies in the shuttle hangars, muzzies in the stalls."

Silly, yes. But it *did* rhyme.

"Oh my! Oh mu-zzeey!" he wailed as he leaned back and spread both arms wide. "I tell you true, I must confess, nothing's been the same since Miko's Muzzy Mess!"

"Stop." But I had to giggle. Mir could be funny sometimes. Almost made me forget about worrying.

"Oh yeah. It's Miko's Muzzy—"

"No more." I waved my hand. "This is serious."

"Serious? How is this serious? Everybody on the station has a muzzy."

I stroked Wuzzy Muzzy, who purred into my ear. True.

"People love 'em, except for one or two grumpy tekkies," Mir went on. "It's a craze, like zipsuits or robotic dogs. We should be selling them. We could make a fortune!"

He had started humming his silly song again when we finally stepped into lab 03. We both stared.

Oh dear.

"Uh, Mir?" I whispered.

"Yeah." He had to see what I saw.

"You wanted to know how this is serious? *This* is serious."

What else could you call it? Everywhere you looked, blue and yellow muzzies piled up on the tables. Red and green muzzies crawled over one another on the floor. Orange and purple muzzies wiggled across the piles of electronic gizmos the tekkies were working on. (Or trying to work on.)

"Finally!" cried a blue-suited tech over in the corner. He brushed a muzzy from his computer. "Are you here to take these things away?"

We nodded. Mir and I looked at each other.

"We need a bigger room to keep them all in," I whispered.

Nightmare, Part Two

8

Buzz was the one who thought of keeping the muzzies in one of the shuttle hangars. So by Day 07 of the Muzzy Mess, we had managed to bring them all over to their new home in boxes. We tied screens over the tops to keep them inside. (Remember, things in the shuttle hangars are weightless.)

"Here you go," sighed DeeBee.

"Rrrooo?"

I wished I knew what the muzzies were saying. Not that it would do us any good, but it would have been fun to know.

"Rrrrooo? Rrrrooo-ooo?" They chattered nonstop.

I sat down, right in between all the boxes. My gripper shoes held me to the floor.

"I think that's it, Miko." DeeBee smiled at me. "I think we got them all."

I nodded and leaned back. She was probably right. But I noticed the muzzies were acting antsier and antsier every hour. Some of them were turning over and wiggling around.

"Looks as if their backs are itchy," I told the others. No one answered—I think everyone was a little tired of muzzies by that time. We had stopped counting after 9,999.

Did I mention muzzies were noisy? I think that is what woke me up two mornings later, Day 09 of the Muzzy Mess.

Thump. Thump.

I lay on my anti-grav mat, dreaming about looking for muzzies. I was truly hoping we had found them all by that time. I thought we had.

Suddenly I woke up. Silence. No "rrroooo." Nothing except DeeBee's snoring and the usual soft *hummm* of the station. Not too many people were awake at 0600.

"Wuzzy?" I felt the little box under my bunk, where Wuzzy Muzzy always slept. DeeBee's dad had let me keep Wuzzy, since I promised to take care of him and keep him out of trouble.

No Wuzzy Muzzy.

Uh-oh. I switched off the invisible blanket field that covered me and kept me warm. Then I went out to explore.

THUMP!

At first I thought someone was knocking on our door. But who would do that so early?

THUMP! BUMP! WHUMP!

There it was again, behind me, in the next room. Was that what woke me up?

CRASH! BASH! MASH!

A moment later, the light panels brightened up. Before long, everyone was awake.

"What's going on, Miko?" DeeBee rubbed the sleep from her eyes. We both ran out into the hallway to see. And then something hit me in the back of the head.

"Hi-YAH!" I yelled. I spun with both hands ready.

You should know that I have never hurt anyone. (Do not tell that to any bad guys, please.) But I *am* fairly good at flipping and tossing people over my head.

Flip!

Toss!

That is what I might have done.

Only who was there to flip and toss?

"Whoa." DeeBee whistled through her teeth. "What kind of butterflies are these?"

Butterflies? The muzzies had sprouted wings! Too bad they were not very good at using them.

Now, I wouldn't want to hurt their feelings. I would probably fly just as poorly if I were trying out my new wings. Remember how hard it was when you flew your first space scooter?

"They're so cute!" DeeBee pulled me to the side as a flock of flying muzzies brushed by our heads. "But how did they get out?"

Swoosh!

This reminded me of the time when Mir had taken over all the station drones.

Only this was worse.

How much worse?

Ker-SMASH! A flying muzzy hit a control panel

on the wall and sent sparks flying. Ouch! That had to hurt. But he just shook his poor little head and kept flying in crazy circles.

How much worse?

BASH! BOSH! BEESH! Three more flying muzzies tumbled in behind him. Their brightly colored wings tangled together until they untied themselves.

Are you still wondering?

THUNK! CRASH! I counted twenty-five more of them, aiming for a skylight window near the ceiling. It reminded me of a whole school of meteors plunking into the moon. That is why the moon has craters, you know.

Ka-PLUNK! Ker-PLOW! One after the other.

Wacko station drones were nothing compared to this!

QUESTION 08:

All this trouble from butterflies?

ANSWER 08:

Remember, they are not butterflies. They are a lot bigger. At first, I called them "flying

muzzies," but that was too long, too hard to say. Muzziflies? That was even worse. Flyzees?

"Ahhh!" Tag ran screaming down the hall behind us. He was still wearing his *Star Bores* pajamas, the ones with pictures of people in strange costumes, waving long flashlights. "I just wanted to see—"

"See what?" DeeBee asked.

"I just went to see how the muzzies were doing, and all these, these flying muzzies . . . fl-fl-lumzies . . . all came whooshing out through the door!"

That would be the door to shuttle hangar 02. Not the outside door, you understand, but the inside door. They must have found a way to fly out of their boxes.

"Tag!" yelled his sister. "Wait a minute!"

Tag didn't stop. He kept running down the hall. At least he had named them for us. *Flumzies.* But we could hardly walk down the hallway without being hit by the clumsy flumzies and their floppy wings. Not to mention the ones who were still muzzies—they had gotten out, too.

The flumzies were still cute, of course. I could

tell they didn't mean to hit things. But this was way out of control.

"What do we do now?" I wondered out loud. Thousands of muzzies had turned into thousands of flumzies.

BAA . . . BAA . . . BAAA! A warning bell went off, and the overhead lights flashed red. That was not the answer I had wanted to my question.

⑨ Station Alert! ✳ ✳ ✳

"Warning!" came a recorded woman's voice. "Station Alert! Station Alert!"

"DeeBee!" Another voice cut through all the warnings and buzzers. "DeeBee Ortiz!"

DeeBee and I looked at each other. DeeBee's eyes grew big, and she looked down at the balding head floating above her wrist interface.

Station Commander Chekhov! And he did not look at all happy. Judge for yourself. His station was being attacked by flumzies. His cheeks were puffed out, and his eyes were red. Maybe that was because he had just woken up.

Or maybe we were not so lucky.

"Yes, sir?" DeeBee whispered. I could not remember when the station commander had called DeeBee for anything.

"I want you and your AstroKids friends to meet

me in the control room." He ducked. I think a flumzy flew by his head. *"Right now!"*

"Y-yes, sir," answered DeeBee. "ASAP."

As Soon As Possible.

I could only gulp. Because now everybody would find out this whole muzzy mess was my fault.

And when they did, it was good-bye, *CLEO*-7.

"Don't worry, Miko." DeeBee patted my shoulder and looked around. Maybe she had guessed what I was thinking. "Remember what Jesus said about worrying? Everything's going to be fine."

I was not sure "fine" was the right word to use. *Terrible, awful, horrible,* or *grim,* perhaps. Anything but "fine."

At least Zero-G was having fun. He was running up and down the hallway, hopping and chasing every flumzy he could find.

"I say, wait there, little flying thing!" He missed another one. "Wouldn't you like to play chase? Tell all your friends to come here."

Tell all your friends?

That gave me an idea!

Could we make it work? Maybe. Now, I am no genius, not like DeeBee. But every once in a great while, I come up with a pretty good idea. If I could only get someone to help me do it. . . .

The Wise Space Sayings of Miko Sato, Number 03

"Two heads are . . .
. . . pretty scary."

In this case, two heads thinking about my plan turned out to be a good thing. I talked to DeeBee. I even asked Zero-G about it. They both thought my idea might work. But I was still worried as our station commander paced in front of us in the control room.

"Do any of you kids know how serious this is?" he asked. He batted an orange flumzy away from his face.

"Yes, sir." DeeBee and Buzz answered for the rest of us. We knew Station Commander Chekhov was going to tell us how the flumzies were wrecking *CLEO-7.* "But Miko has an—"

He put up his hand for them not to interrupt.

"Now, I know you kids wanted to collect all these, er, muzzo—"

"Muzzies," Mir corrected his father.

"And flumzies," added Tag. "That's what we call the ones that have wings."

The commander shook his head. "Flying fuzzies, whatever. I know you've wanted to collect them as pets. But it's too late for that now. So I'm ordering them trapped and released—outside."

"But—" I bit my lip. This was the end.

Commander Chekhov turned to look at me. Was he going to send me back to the moon?

I held up my finger. "Excuse me, sir, but . . ."

He raised his bushy eyebrows.

It would be now or never. I took a deep breath.

"I have an idea how we can get all the, ah, flumzies together without hurting them."

"You do?"

"Yes, sir."

He stared at me, pressed his lips together, and waited for me to finish.

I took another deep breath.

"Here's what I think we can do. . . ."

Save the Muzzies

You understand by now I am not the techno-genius of *CLEO-7*. But I really thought my idea might work. After our showdown with Commander Chekhov, we AstroKids went back to DeeBee's shop to get ready. He had given us two hours to try my idea; we had to work quickly.

"Problem is," said Buzz, "some of them are still muzzies, but—"

"Most of them have turned into flumzies!" Tag finished his sentence.

"And a lot of them are still flying around," DeeBee said. "They're wrecking everything in the station."

"But some are hiding in the walls!" Tag did not want to be left out. "And who knows what *they're* eating."

Oh, things were a mess, all right. Especially with hungry muzzies and flumzies nibbling on anything soft and chewy. It didn't matter if it was food! If they were really, really hungry, they even ate things like wires, zipsuits, and power relays. You can understand why the grown-ups were so upset.

Which brings me to . . .

The Wise Space Sayings of Miko Sato, Number 04

"It's always darkest . . .

. . . just before you flunk a test."

This was some test, and I wasn't sure I would pass.

"Whatever we do, kids, it had better be done quickly." Zero-G paced at our feet.

"Because if we don't"—MAC's lights blinked in double-time—"Station Commander Chekhov is going to start, er, *disposing* of the poor muzzies in one hour, fifty-six minutes, and twelve seconds."

I did not like that word at all—"disposing." But MAC was right. The commander had given us two hours, no more.

"We should go, then, Mir." I looked at my watch.

Five minutes later, Mir and I stood in front of a drone control station in hall 37-G. In case you are wondering, a drone control station looks like a flat box on the wall, not much bigger than you or me. All its lights were off.

"This is where I saw a family of muzzies—right there." Mir pointed. "It sounded like they were talking to one another."

"I think they ate through the controls." I shook my head.

We knelt by a jagged hole and listened.

"Do you think they'll still be hungry enough?" he asked.

"Are you kidding?" I checked my palm recorder before I gave it to Mir. "Just make sure you hit Record."

My job was to hold the bait, and I checked my pocket for the one chocolate bar Commander Chekhov had allowed us to use.

"Hello, muzzy, muzzy," I called. "You can come out. We are not going to hurt you."

"They haven't been shy before." Mir bent down next to me.

I unwrapped the chocolate and waved it next to the hole.

"Come out, come out, wherever you are . . ."

Not five seconds later, I hear scratching noises coming from inside the control station. Closer, closer . . .

WHOMP! The muzzies attacked my chocolate.

"Rrrooooooooo!" said one.

"Rrrrrrrrooooo-rrooooo!" said another.

I was lucky to pull my hand away in time.

"I'm sorry, guys," I whispered. "I promise we'll give you a real dinner soon."

Hungry little creatures, those.

"Did you get all those 'rroos'?" I asked Mir.

He smiled and punched a button on the palm recorder. "Let's go."

That meant "yes."

We ran back to DeeBee's shop.

I caught my breath. "Is it going to work?"

"Relax. It'll work." DeeBee wiped a bead of sweat from her forehead. Her job was to hook up our recorder to five mobile speakers we could carry around the station. "I just don't know if it'll work in time."

I did not need to hear that last comment.

"Let's go!" I told everyone.

"Let's go?" DeeBee looked up from her work and gulped. "But I haven't tested it yet. We don't know for sure if muzzies speak the same language as flumzies."

I knew what she meant. But what else could we do?

"Mistress Miko?" Zero-G scratched at my leg, trying to get my attention.

"I'm terribly sorry, boy," I told him. "You are going to have to wait."

"Miko's right," said Buzz. He scooped up his wireless speaker and headed out the door. "There's no time. We'll have to test it as we go."

We started out as far away from shuttle hangar 02 as we could. We guessed there were thousands of flumzies all over the station now, plus a few hundred muzzies. Maybe more.

And whether they had wings or not, they were all hungry. We were counting on it for this plan to work.

Pied Piper of
11 Muzzyland

✳ ✳ ✳

"Speakers ready?" DeeBee asked from her perch on lookout deck 22.

Mir, Tag, and Buzz gave the thumbs-up sign. I nodded. If this worked, muzzies and flumzies would be able to hear our message everywhere. We would run through the dining room. The rec center. The shops. The control center. We would even run past the apartments where people lived.

"Please, could we turn it up double?" I asked.

Everyone looked at me as if I were crazy. But DeeBee thought it was a good idea. She turned it up triple.

"Yeah, rock on." Tag smiled.

I checked the time we had left as Zero-G pawed at my leg.

"Hit the switch, DeeBee!" Buzz gave the order. She did.

We all looked at each other. What did we expect, some kind of explosion?

No such luck. All we heard was the humming of the station. That, and a couple of crashes as clumsy flumzies did more damage.

"I cannot hear anything." Tag scrunched his nose.

DeeBee frowned back. "Wait a minute." She pressed the switch a couple more times, and then . . .

"Rrroooooooo!"

I could feel it in the floor, quietly rumbling under my feet. Rumbling my bones, for that matter. Muzzy talk. Getting louder.

"Yeah!" Tag held his ears.

"They're hearing it now." DeeBee smiled.

I hoped she was right. And I hoped the muzzy that had jumped on my chocolate bar had said something like "Mmmm, chocolate! Eat!"

QUESTION 09:
    What if it had? What then?

Answer 09:

This plan was supposed to work better than an ouchless mousetrap. If the muzzies heard "chocolate," we hoped they would come check it out for themselves. That's exactly what happens when Mir's mother calls "Dinner is served!" And just like Mir, these little animals are always hungry!

Tag looked around a couple of minutes later. There was plenty of rumbling, but no muzzies or flumzies. "I don't think it's working."

"Come on, Tag," Mir scolded him. "Have some faith."

"Perhaps you should turn it up," I said as we walked slowly down one more hall with our wireless speakers.

But DeeBee shook her head. "It's already up full blast."

Zero-G was dancing in circles, barking. "Mistress Miko, I think you should know—"

"Not *now*, boy!" I told him.

That is when I heard a tumbling sound. A roar,

like the blaster engines on a shuttle. Or a waterfall, back on Earth.

Tag's eyes grew big. A wall panel crashed to the floor behind us.

"Don't look now," Buzz warned us as he turned around. "But here they come!"

Yikes! The air was filled with red, blue, yellow, and green flumzies . . . all coming right at us!

"Run!" cried Tag.

Now the fun *really* began. Picture thousands of flumzies coming out of cracks in the walls and dropping out of air vents.

Ker-PLOP, PLOP, PLOP, PLOP!

Then picture a flock of swarming flumzies, circling over your head.

We still were not exactly sure what the recording was telling the flumzies, over and over. But whatever it was, it was working. After all . . .

The Wise Space Sayings of Miko Sato, Number 05

"Haste makes . . .

. . . sweat."

We worked up a pretty good sweat, hurrying up and down the hallways of *CLEO-7*. We had to make sure all the flumzies and muzzies heard us.

"This way!" Buzz told us. He waved us past the labs.

"Over here!" Mir found another way. Our goal: shuttle hangar 02, the only place in the station we could store all those animals.

Yippy-i-o, cowboy! Talk about roundups. This was turning out to be the greatest muzzy-flumzy roundup in history!

Shall I make a long story short? We ran up and down every single hall in *CLEO-7*, rounding up muzzies and flumzies. Every lab. Every control room. Every apartment. Every storage closet. An hour later, we all stood together in shuttle hangar 02, gasping for breath.

"Can you believe it?" Tag was beaming. You would have thought his spaceball team just won the Solar System Series. He gave me a galaxy salute, where you hook little fingers and shake. "I'll keep the door closed this time."

"Good job, Miko!" DeeBee turned to me with a hug. "You did it."

"*We* did it." I corrected her. We had herded every last muzzy and flumzy into the shuttle hangar. I bet not even Commander Chekhov dreamed how many muzzies and flumzies we had. Believe me, you would not want to count them.

"Yee-haw!" said space cowboy Tag.

Mir and Buzz slapped each other on the back. But then their smiles faded, like the sun setting on Earth.

Oh dear.

We could not keep all those critters there in shuttle hangar 02. If we did, the commander would just say thank you very much, open the outside doors, and whoosh them out.

Now what?

Worry and more worry!

Ms. E. Clips
12 Takes Charge   ✳ ✳ ✳

For about the fourth time in the past hour, Zero-G pushed at me with his nose and dug at my foot.

"I say, Mistress Miko! Please let me tell you something!"

I looked down at the little dog. "Tell me what?"

"I saw a moon shuttle land in the other shuttle hangar, not long ago. And there's a woman on board who's been looking for you."

"For me?"

"Well, I'm not sure, but I think so."

I caught my breath. My heart stopped. My mouth went dry.

Actually, moon shuttles came to *CLEO-7* all the time. But if someone wanted to see me, well, that could mean only one thing.

And it was not good.

"As I said, I'm not sure, Mistress Miko." Zero-G took a moment to scratch his ear. "But she and the commander have been looking around. I heard them mention your name."

Everyone huddled around me. They had to know what I was thinking.

DeeBee rested her hand on my shoulder again. "We won't let anyone from the Children's Home take you away, Miko."

"Right," agreed Buzz. "You've got a place here. A new life."

"Rrrooo," said all the flumzies and muzzies.

That made me feel a little better. Only problem was, just feeling better was not going to be enough. I needed somewhere to hide. But I had run out of time.

Even above the animal noise, we could hear the woman's voice at the door. "Oh, look at this. We've finally found them!"

At first, I thought perhaps I would know who it was. But I had never seen this woman before. She wore a pink jumpsuit and came at us with her arms open wide. Station Commander Chekhov followed right behind.

Yes, it was too late to run. So I crossed my arms and waited. The rest of the AstroKids circled around me, like bodyguards.

"I'll kick her in the leg," whispered Tag.

"I could be asked to bite her foot," Zero-G added.

"Warning! Warning!" said MAC.

"Hush." DeeBee held them back.

"This is remarkable," bubbled the woman. She looked around the big shuttle hangar, filled with thousands of flumzies and muzzies. "Simply remarkable."

I had seen that kind of toothy smile before. They flash it before they grab you and take you away.

"I'm sorry you came all this way for nothing." Buzz stepped up to meet her. "But Miko wants to stay here. She doesn't want to go back to the moon."

This was nice of Buzz. Quite nice. But I felt odd, hiding behind him and the other AstroKids.

Commander Chekhov stepped up. "Kids, this is Ms. E. Clips," he told us. "She's from the Lunar Research Laboratory."

The other kids all looked at me. What? The Lunar Research Lab?

"You aren't from the Apollo Children's Home?" I whispered.

She looked at me and laughed.

"Heavens, no, child. I came as soon as I heard you had found our two stolen muzzo-lumpiriri."

"You mean to say, these are *your* muzzies?"

"Well, in a way." She looked around. "We'd been trying at the lab for months to raise muzzo-lumpiriri. Only we never could. Nothing ever worked. And now, here, in no time at all, look what you've done! Dr. Muzzolump is going to be *thrilled!*"

Commander Chekhov beamed.

So did everyone else.

And I had to admit it: DeeBee had been right

about not worrying.

"It was kind of an accident," I said.

We explained everything to Ms. E. Clips, from the time we first found the muzzies, to the time I fed them chocolate, to the time they started turning into flumzies, and more.

Ms. E. Clips wanted to know exactly what kind of chocolate we fed the first two muzzies. Was there something special about it? Why didn't it make them sick?

I told her about the old Blast-Off Chocolate Bar, and about the old chocolate under Tag's bed. She thought maybe there was something different about our chocolate.

"Yeah, we carry ours in our pockets for months!" Tag laughed.

Ms. E. Clips said she would look into it. Who could say?

It turns out the muzzies were being raised as pets for people on long, boring space flights. And they were quite valuable. Ms. E. Clips was going to take them all back with her in her Lunar Research Lab shuttle.

"I am sorry. Did you say *all* of them?" I asked. That would be quite a trick. Even so, we told Ms. E. Clips we would gladly help her load them into her shuttle.

"Or maybe we could put some in a space scooter for you," said Tag. "We could even race you! Yeah, that's a great idea. A race to the moon. Or maybe Mars!"

That sounded like another wild adventure to me. Uh-oh.

"No, Tag." DeeBee squashed that idea.

But he wasn't giving up. "Well, would you like to borrow a holo-vid for the trip? It's—"

"No!" DeeBee and I yelled together. "Not *Star Wreck*!"

During all the talking, Wuzzy Muzzy found his way back to my shoulder. He curled up his little wings and purred in my ear.

"Wuzzy!" I said. Then I looked at Ms. E. Clips. "Does he have to go, too?"

"Well . . ." Ms. E. Clips laughed. "I think maybe we can spare one or two. As long as—"

"As long as no one feeds them any more old Blast-Off Chocolate Bars," said MAC.

We all laughed.

Right, I thought. *Not even a nibble!*

RealSpace Debrief

✳ ✳ ✳

The AstroKids' Guide to Muzzies and Other Weird Experiments

Are muzzies real?

Sorry, but no! No one has ever tried to cross a fuzzy caterpillar with a cute hamster. Even if they had, it wouldn't work. One's an insect, the other a mammal.

But space is a great place for all kinds of terrific experiments. You never know what you might find out. Take the *Apollo* space program, for instance. Maybe you know men first walked on the moon in 1969. But did you know that today's sport shoes are so good because of what we learned from the first space suits?

That's just one example. About thirteen

hundred *Apollo* ideas have helped make everyday life better. Things like:

- cordless power tools—Got some in your garage? They were first made for *Apollo*.
- water purifiers—The filters that kill bad stuff in our drinking water were first made for moon trips.
- freeze-dried foods—These were invented for moon astronauts. Now you can take them backpacking or wherever!
- CAT scanners—These special machines take pictures of the inside of our bodies, like X rays. Their beginnings were in cameras first used to take pictures of the moon.

Think that's neat? The list gets even longer when you look at all the cool inventions that have come from space-shuttle missions, too. Things like:

- artificial hearts—Teeny-tiny pumps were first made for pumping shuttle fuel. Now these mechanical hearts are helping to save the lives of people who need new hearts.

- lightweight arms and legs—A foam that covered shuttle fuel tanks is now used to make prosthetic, or fake, arms and legs much more comfortable to wear and use.
- lifesaver lights—Scientists tried using a different kind of light to grow plants on the space shuttle. Turns out it was good for helping treat kids for cancer!
- flame-finding cameras—Shuttle pilots used a special camera to watch for flames. Now firefighters back on Earth use it to find forest fires.

The list goes on. A super-camera built for taking pictures of Mars helped museum workers at the Smithsonian Institute clean and fix up the famous old "Star-Spangled Banner"—the flag we sing about in our national anthem.

And don't forget the "e-nose." Really! Remember when Zero-G said the AstroKids should use MAC's "e-sniffer"? Well, that kind of nose is almost a reality today. Space scientists are working on an e-nose that will be able to smell the air inside spaceships. Why? For safety. If fuel or anything else ever starts to leak, the e-nose can let us know, fast!

Which only goes to show that space dreams are turning into real life . . . sooner than we think!

Want to find out more about e-noses and other neat space inventions? Then check out a great Web site for kids, called "The Space Place." The address is *http://spaceplace.jpl.nasa.gov*. You can do space experiments, discover amazing space facts, and lots more.

Also check out:

- neat discoveries from the shuttle (*www.sti.nasa.gov/tto/shuttle.htm*)
- what the moon program gave us (*www.sti.nasa.gov/tto/apollo.htm*)
- *Inventions From Outer Space: Everyday Uses for NASA Technology* by David Baker (Random House, 2000). Not exactly written for kids, but interesting.

And the Coded
Message Is... ✳ ✳ ✳

You think this ASTROKIDS adventure is over? Not yet! Here's the plan: We'll give you the directions, you find the words. Write them all on a piece of paper. They form a secret message that has to do with *Miko's Muzzy Mess*. If you think you got it right, log on to *www.bethanyhouse.com* and follow the instructions there. You'll receive free ASTRO-KIDS wallpaper for your computer and a sneak peek at the next ASTROKIDS adventure. It's that simple!

WORD 1:
chapter 7, paragraph 1, word 3 _____

WORD 2:
chapter 11, paragraph 11, word 2 _____

WORD 3:
chapter 5, paragraph 1, word 56 _____

WORD 4:
chapter 12, paragraph 1, word 5 _____

WORD 5:
chapter 5, paragraph 1, word 19 _____

WORD 6:
chapter 9, paragraph 7, word 5 _____

WORD 7:
chapter 12, paragraph 13, word 11 _____

WORD 8:
chapter 1, paragraph 23, word 5 _____

WORD 9:
chapter 7, paragraph 25, word 17 _____

WRITE IT ALL HERE:

_____

_____

(Hint: Miko says to check out Matthew 6 in the Bible.)

Contact Us! ✳ ✳ ✳

If you have any questions for the author or would just like to say hi, feel free to contact him at Bethany House Publishers, 11400 Hampshire Avenue South, Minneapolis, MN 55438, United States of America, EARTH. Please include a self-addressed, stamped envelope if you'd like a reply. Or log on to Robert's intergalactic Web site at *www.coolreading.com.*

Launch Countdown

✳ ✳ ✳

AstroKids 05:
About-Face Space Race

Who's going to win the great "Martian Mega-Marathon"? Probably the cocky Deeter Meteor from nearby *CLEO-5* . . . unless Tag and the AstroKids can stop him!

But how? At first, Tag thinks his sister DeeBee has a chance. She can build anything (including space scooters). Or maybe Mir, whose parents just bought him a flashy new Omega 22 scooter.

Pretty soon, it's boys against girls, a race to get ready for the big day. And Tag's right in the middle of it all.

Fun? Sure—until Tag finds out what it *really* takes to win. Then it's up to him to convince the rest of the AstroKids—before it's too late!

TRAILBLAZER BOOKS

from Dave and Neta Jackson

TRAILBLAZER BOOKS give kids an adventure story as they learn about Christian heroes from our past.

The books present history, adventure, and stories of faith under one cover. Authors Dave and Neta Jackson span the globe and travel through history to present thrilling stories of missionaries, theologians, doctors, and civil rights leaders who've allowed their faith to change the world.

⬧ BETHANYHOUSE

From Bethany House Publishers

Series for Beginning Readers*

YOUNG COUSINS MYSTERIES®
by Elspeth Campbell Murphy
Rib-tickling mysteries just for beginning readers—with Timothy, Titus, and Sarah-Jane from the THREE COUSINS DETECTIVE CLUB.®

WATCH OUT FOR JOEL!
by Sigmund Brouwer
Seven-year-old Joel is always getting into scrapes—despite his older brother, Ricky, always being told, "Watch out for Joel!"

Series for Young Readers†

ASTROKIDS™
by Robert Elmer
Space scooters? Floating robots? Jupiter ice cream? Blast into the future for out-of-this-world, zero-gravity fun with the AstroKids on space station *CLEO-7.*

THE CUL-DE-SAC KIDS
by Beverly Lewis
Each story in this lighthearted series features the hilarious antics and predicaments of nine endearing boys and girls who live on Blossom Hill Lane.

JANETTE OKE'S ANIMAL FRIENDS
by Janette Oke
Endearing creatures from the farm, forest, and zoo discover their place in God's world through various struggles, mishaps, and adventures.

THREE COUSINS DETECTIVE CLUB®
by Elspeth Campbell Murphy
Famous detective cousins Timothy, Titus, and Sarah-Jane learn compelling Scripture-based truths while finding—and solving—intriguing mysteries.

*(ages 6–8)   †(ages 7–10)

Series for Middle Graders* From BHP

THE ACCIDENTAL DETECTIVES · by Sigmund Brouwer
Action-packed adventures lead Ricky Kidd and his friends into places they never dreamed of, drawing them closer with every step.

ADVENTURES DOWN UNDER · by Robert Elmer
When Patrick McWaid's father is unjustly sent to Australia as a prisoner in 1867, the rest of the family follows, uncovering action-packed mystery along the way.

ADVENTURES OF THE NORTHWOODS · by Lois Walfrid Johnson
Kate O'Connell and her stepbrother Anders encounter mystery and adventure in northwest Wisconsin near the turn of the century.

BLOODHOUNDS, INC. · by Bill Myers
Hilarious, hair-raising suspense follows brother-and-sister detectives Sean and Melissa Hunter in these madcap mysteries with a message.

GIRLS ONLY! · by Beverly Lewis
Four talented young athletes become fast friends as together they pursue their Olympic dreams.

MANDIE BOOKS · by Lois Gladys Leppard
With over five million sold, the turn-of-the-century adventures of Mandie and her many friends will keep readers eager for more.

PROMISE OF ZION · by Robert Elmer
Following WWII, thirteen-year-old Dov Zalinsky leaves for Palestine—the one place he may still find his parents—and meets the adventurous Emily Parkinson. Together they experience the dangers of life in the Holy Land.

THE RIVERBOAT ADVENTURES · by Lois Walfrid Johnson
Libby Norstad and her friend Caleb face the challenges and risks of working with the Underground Railroad during the mid–1800s.

TRAILBLAZER BOOKS · by Dave and Neta Jackson
Follow the exciting lives of real-life Christian heroes through the eyes of child characters as they share their faith with others around the world.

THE YOUNG UNDERGROUND · by Robert Elmer
Peter and Elise Andersen's plots to protect their friends and themselves from Nazi soldiers in World War II Denmark guarantee fast-paced action and suspenseful reads.

*(ages 8–13)